An Affair with Mr Renoir

An Affair with Mr Renoir

A collection of stories by
Tessa Bremner

Acknowledgements

Thank you, Ian, for hearing my stories and my ideas,
Malcolm for introducing me to his publisher,
Stephen and Stella for proofreading,
and Suzanna for the artwork.

Thank you as well to the many women who inspired me.

An Affair with Mr Renoir
ISBN 978 1 74027 236 0
Copyright © Tessa Bremner 2003
Cover image (*You Make Me Want To Wear Dresses*) by Suzanne Moss

First published 2003
Reprinted 2016

GINNINDERRA PRESS
PO Box 3461 Port Adelaide 5015
www.ginninderrapress.com.au

Contents

An Affair with Mr Renoir

We sit looking at each other across the dinner table. The four of us are easy together. We've been friends for a long time. Here in our English village, our friendship gives us solace. Up in London, we always have to rush and there is no time for conversation. Silence here between us is not something to be rectified. It is comforting.

We talk of painting and exhibitions. They all know and tease me lovingly for my keen interest in painting. Laughing along, I think of the paintings upstairs that I have recently created with such intensity. No one has seen them, not even Edward, with whom I have lived for twenty-four years. He earns the money that puts the bread on our table. Artistic enjoyment is limited to an occasional visit to the Tate.

'Catherine's going to Paris next month,' he tells our friends over dinner. 'Her sister, Cicely, has gone there to live. I thought it would be nice for her to have a little holiday.'

I have never been to Paris. I have never even been to France, except for a weekend in Cherbourg that we took not long after we were married. Edward often goes. He brings back perfume, redolent with romance and quiet dreams that infiltrate my mind. The aromatic headiness leads me to fantasies of creative blossoming.

I have never been with – or, as the Bible says, known – another man. Edward has been my life. I have always been there for him and every part of the house and garden has a connecting string that holds me to him. Red roses here, because he loves that colour, pansies in a patch there and a white border that is the envy of all our friends. In my garden, the first artistic stirrings were felt. One spring day when Edward was at work, I started to draw the flowers that were opening their petals. In time, I moved from pencil to crayon and then to oils. Finally I joined the art society and with staid and cultured ladies I journeyed to London to see exhibitions. Afterwards, I would meet Edward and he would take me to dinner and tease me about what he called my hobby.

I didn't tell him that my heart had caught on fire in a way that I had never experienced before. When the bloom of a flower or the movement of wind took hold in a painting, I was gripped by excitement. Rodney, my teacher, encouraged me. He said I had talent and a style that was unique.

Edward didn't like that. He started to be jealous, first of the teacher and then of my painting. 'Darling,' he said, 'you have enough to do without this silliness. Why don't you redecorate the drawing room? You choose the colours and you can use your artistic skills to make it look lovely.' He kissed me gently and left the house to catch the train.

I redecorated the room. I put one of my paintings in a corner, elegantly framed and unsigned. Edward admired my taste. I told him it was by an emerging new talent, a man. I'd read it was worth investing in his work. It pleased Edward to hear me being practical.

I concealed a new feeling that was taking me by surprise. It simmered inside like the curry that was cooked the day before a dinner party and then was reheated with extra spices and herbs. It changed colour and at times I felt that my face might reflect the blue, then purple and red that I felt. I went to art classes and threw these new feelings into my work.

I was confused. I was still in love, but how could my painting stand in the way of my feelings for Edward?

'Her brother-in-law's got some flash diplomatic position there,' explains Edward. 'I'm going to join her the following week when the two girls have talked themselves out. Bit of shopping…'

'Catherine,' says Monica, 'there's a Renoir exhibition on there. You should go to see it.' Only Monica knows and cares for my painting.

'If she wants, she can go and dabble in the shadow of Renoir's glory,' says Edward, and he and Michael launch into student memories of time spent in Paris.

Monica looks at me. I smile my best I-am-in-front-of-guests smile but I long to spoon the crème brûlée over his head. Maybe this is another face of love, I think. Monica winks. It trivialises my passion. I'm glad

I haven't shown Monica my recent work. It would probably shock her and the winks would be flattened out.

After I have put the dishes in the machine and tidied the kitchen, I go up to bed. Edward is happy with the evening. The meal was delicious and he and Michael have made plans for a new investment. He feels successful. We make love. Edward is a considerate lover. He taught me all I know about sex. Recently I have been looking at Picasso sketches and some Japanese erotic art that Mary showed me during art class. Mary is divorced and having an affair. She thinks I'm naïve. Ignorant, more likely. I saw things I'd never imagined and I suppose neither has Edward. We go along the same path each time. It never varies. Out of my timid orgasm sprang two healthy and beautiful children. My orgasm has never intensified. It is almost a duty now to come to the count. It indulges Edward's ego. I do it and I dream of my painting as I listen to Edward's quiet panting leading to his final thrust.

'Darling,' he whispers, though there is no one in the house to hear.

It must be because we are just over the finishing line of sex. Like in church, people after sex whisper as if they have just tasted the bread and wine, but during, they shout and sing. No. I have never raised my voice, but Edward sometimes does. A kind of primordial grunt.

'Darling, why don't you go to the Renoir exhibition. It would be good for you.'

My heart hovers crazily in anticipation of new words.

'It might help you see the reality of your ability. Good night sweet heart.' He kisses me gently.

Is this what love is, I wonder again.

Rodney leans over me as I put the finishing touches to the portrait I am painting. 'You're ready for an exhibition,' he says.

He smells of garlic and herbs and, under his breath, of exotic food. I feel conventional and ordinary. He wears jeans that have smears of paint.

'Why doesn't he get a proper job?' Edward remarked when he met him after class one day.

Rodney has beautiful hands that I want to paint. I want to take them home with me. Hands fascinate me. I saw a photo of a cellist's hands and I felt a desire to be the cello, to be fingered and song-spun until my head was giddy.

'I'm not good enough,' I say to Rodney.

He persists. 'What's stopping you?'

He looks into my eyes and my breath stops. He is challenging my confidence and he is provoking Edward. Except Edward doesn't know, but he will detect the excitement of the dream Rodney's words have manifested in me.

'Start working towards an exhibition,' Rodney says.

On my way home, I meet Monica. I have paint on my cheek and she wipes it off with her handkerchief.

'I have a book for you,' and hands me a large illustrated copy of the paintings of Renoir. 'Get to know them,' she advises. 'You'll enjoy the exhibition more.'

We have tea together and we turn the pages from one delight to another. I feel comfortable in this world of colour.

'The real thing is better,' she says.

The bodies are beautiful. I see the plump naked women by the river and see the light how it falls. It is as if it is shimmering out of the pages onto my receptive skin. I long to try to paint light in this radiant way.

Next art class, I try experiments with light and Rodney is thrilled. He wants me to meet a friend of his who is coming down from London. I tell Edward, who says that we shall be out of town. I didn't tell him the date, so I know that it is his way of saying no. I tell Rodney I am busy.

He frowns and draws in his breath. 'One day you'll be ready,' he says.

It is Edward's birthday. We have a dinner party to celebrate. Monica and Michael are there of course. So is Mr Peters, the local vicar, and his wife, Felicity. She comes to art classes with me and I hope and pray that she won't talk about it. She does. It's over coffee. We are sitting in the drawing room. Mr Peters admires the decoration.

Edward tells them that I did it. 'I like her to indulge her artistic ability. She's good at decorating.'

Then it comes. 'What about her painting, Edward?' As if I am not there. 'Rodney says she has a rare talent. He thinks she should exhibit, doesn't he.' She looks at me, wreathed in smiles.

I wither.

Later, in bed, Edward says he doesn't think I should go to art classes, as Rodney sounds a bit of a fool. 'How could you ever exhibit?' he says. 'He's filling your head with silly ideas way out of your field. Be your age, Catherine. Be my wife. What's wrong with being my wife? Aren't you happy? Don't I give you enough?' He fires question after question but doesn't wait for a reply.

I don't know how to reply. I shall concede. I turn away and my body burns with resentment. He strokes my back and lovemaking begins. As he penetrates me, I feel my life force leak out. I want to paint, to capture perceptions and keep hold of the tiny remaining strands of creative energy as they spill away in his gasps and cries.

'My funny little chicken,' he says fondly, 'you have such sweet ideas.'

Am I right, I wonder, to believe Edward is the master who holds the wisdom of the world?

'Why do you go on like this listening to a fool like Rodney? He just wants your custom, that's all. Of course he's going to say you're good. I expect he says the same to everyone.'

'I expect so,' I say.

But in the night I wake from a dream of bathing women caught in cascading colour and light. Edward is in the dream and he has a paintbrush. He dips the brush into a pot of paint and slowly and deliberately paints the women away. He blacks the image into nothing. I look at my hands. They start to break up like shattered china. They fall into the box of paints and all are blown away. I wake sweating.

I go to Paris.

'There are lots of things to see in Paris,' says Edward. He tells me that he has rung Geoffrey and suggested some outings that might amuse me. The Eiffel Tower has never been of interest to me. Edward gives me spending money that makes me gasp. I am to go shopping. He has written a list of things he'd like me to buy. 'You'll be busy,' he says. As we kiss goodbye, he adds, 'I'm sure Mr Renoir can manage without you.'

I am thrown into a swirl of traffic, culinary aromas, language and beautiful buildings.

'It's so different from London,' explains Cicely.

'But London was bombed,' I say.

Paris kept its culture intact for its complicity during the war and secretly we are glad that its treasures are still here.

Cicely tells me her husband Geoffrey has been speaking to Edward quite a lot recently. 'Catherine, Edward seemed upset. Do you mind telling me? Are you having an affair?'

I laugh. If I'm having an affair, then it is with a tube of paint and my brush. I explain to Cicely how Edward hates me painting. Cicely laughs; she is relieved and amused. I will not shame her or Geoffrey.

The traffic is slow. As we pass the Arc de Triomphe, the evening sun is caught in golden shafts of light. I wish for my sketchbook.

We plan to go shopping. I tell Cicely that I'd like to shop on my own and browse. We arrange to meet for lunch. She drives me to the centre and I enter a parfumerie near the Opera. I buy some scent for me and aftershave for Edward. I do not browse. I rush out and hail a taxi.

I have exactly one hour and thirty-five minutes and I am paying to get into the gallery. In five minutes I shall be in front of his Nude in the Sunlight. It is more wonderful than I could ever imagine. His use of light is exactly what Rodney had told me. If I stand close it is just paint, but if I move away it bursts into splendour. Next to it two girls are at a piano. They look comfortable in a luscious and gentle light that bathes it. I feel that I am in the room. I walk backwards without taking my eyes from the painting.

I thought I was on my own and am surprised when I turn to see a man with an amused expression on his face watching me.

'Renoir has that effect on many people when they see his painting for the first time.' He is a man who might be in his sixties. He has lots of thick, greying hair and a kind face. He is elegantly dressed in a European way.

'How do you know it's my first time and how did you know I speak English?' I ask.

'Your body. I think you were in that painting, standing by the piano. You were so tense and excited and, to answer the second part of your question, I guessed.' He laughs.

We move comfortably together to a painting in which two girls sit looking out at an exquisite view. The picture is permeated with warmth. A summer's day. They have been picking wild flowers. He asks me what I think they are doing, sitting there. I tell him that the blonde girl is pondering life. She sees its bloom in the flowers before her and knows its brevity. I know myself how little time I have to paint and a surge of longing takes hold of me. I must paint, whatever the consequences. I know so little about painting and I want to absorb everything, but my watch tells me that I have to leave. Like Cinderella, I must run away and be back at the Opera to meet Cicely. I have one bottle of scent and some trifles to show for the ninety minutes spent on my own.

In the taxi, I think of excuses and realise that I am behaving as if I were having an affair. I am planning to lie to the people I love.

'You bought so little in an hour and a half. Poor darling! Was it a language problem?'

They discuss me as if I were a child and make plans for me for the next day. I want only to sit in front of paintings. I try to suggest a visit to the Jeu de Paume Gallery.

I have never been able to speak out for myself. Everybody has always told me what to do, and I have done it. I have never thought of Edward as being domineering, but he is. He is no different from my father, whom I loved. When I was a child, he told me he knew better and I thought he did. I didn't go to university, because he considered it better for me to do something useful and so I did that too. I married Edward and became a slave to his wishes that I believed were my own. He decided where we holidayed, where the children went to school and set me daily chores as if I needed my time filled with a code of Protestant ethics.

'Mum,' Joanna used to tease, 'why do you always do what Dad wants? Haven't you got an idea of your own in your head? You let modern woman down.'

When the children were young, I joined a bell-ringing circle and went once a week. I enjoyed the company. A man called John led the group. He was widely travelled and often brought photographs of recent trips. His wife, a music teacher, had rosy cheeks and a constantly contented expression as if she had a secret understanding of life that eluded the rest of us. I sketched her and then painted her. I loved the rhythm and companionship and the opportunity to sketch movement of the bell-ringers. Edward started going out on the same evening and I had to get a babysitter. The children and he complained and I agreed it would be better not to go any more. Future courses I did during the day, and Edward was satisfied with French cooking, furniture restoration and wallpapering. I was bored.

I threw myself into being a mother and filled the house with friends of Rory and Joanna and cooked colossal meals and listened to complaints and laughter. In the evenings, I changed to welcome Edward back from London. A drink and dinner with new recipes. Maybe I was content. I had everything I could want. Joanna was right. I had no ideas of my own.

Joanna flew through university with a first in languages and is now in India backpacking before going to Australia for a year. She has plenty of ideas on improving the world. Rory is in business in the City. He has a small house in Dulwich and a fiancée. He is kind, conventional and far too fond of money. Both my children expect me to be there for them as I always have been. One day I would be the babysitter to Rory's children and the sounding board for Joanna's complaints about the world on her return.

Geoffrey and Cicely make plans for the next day. A morning spent up the Eiffel Tower and then at Les Invalides. Versailles the following day.

As I fall to sleep, I think of the exhibition and the man who had so kindly talked to me. I don't know his name. I call him Mr Renoir. 'Good night, Mr Renoir,' I whisper to my pillow.

I wake from a dream in which I was in the gallery, standing in front of a Renoir painting which depicted a long flight of steps bathed in sunlight. People were coming down the steps and, when I looked closer, I saw Mr Renoir among them. A noise disturbed me. I turned and saw Edward stride into the gallery. He was furious. He was shouting something about me going against his wishes. I'd never seen him so angry. I was about to move away from the painting, when it came to life. Mr Renoir was running down the steps and reaching his hand out to me. I looked at Edward and his fury and then at Mr Renoir in the golden light of sunshine and warmth. I put my hand in his and he drew me into the picture. I didn't look behind me, but I knew that Edward was watching me as I climbed the stairs.

Next day, I scramble up the steps of the Eiffel Tower to admire the view over Paris. I refuse the lift. I want to experience each level. The wind gets stronger. Climbing the steps is a continuation of my dream. It is taking me into unknown spaces. I wish I could paint the panting of my breath and the confusion of my thoughts. Cicely waits for me at the top, dull in her expensive English suit. As I gasp out into the open, she is brought to life by the blue, hazy light that shimmers on her. The breeze catches her scarf and explodes her neat appearance into colourful abandon. I take out my sketchbook.

'Don't embarrass me,' she says, her mouth a thin, straight line.

My family was not interested in art and any painting on a wall was there by the insistence of an interior decorator. They hung in neat lines; a pretence at culture by colour or theme. A Stubbs hunting scene in my father's office. A still life with a bowl of fruit and a dead hare hung in the kitchen. Edward was happy to continue this perception of art. Cicely followed Geoffrey in his conservative taste.

At Versailles, we walk down the long mirrored hall and I imagine Louis XIV, the Sun King. The tall narrow windows let in braids of light that lace around the naked figures holding huge gold candelabra. Through the window, two small girls are running after each other. A woman remonstrates. A man walks towards the fountain. I watch him. A lopsided lurch hangs in my belly. When Cicely and I go to the fountain, he is sitting on a bench reading.

'Hello again,' he says casually.

I smile, looking into his eyes.

'Who was that?' she wants to know.

I tell her I have no idea.

'He seemed to know you.'

'We met yesterday.'

'Where?'

'I don't remember,' I lie. Why is it important?

'I don't believe you. He looked at you as if he knew you really well. And you – I don't know, Catherine, but you seem secretive and odd.' The way she looks at me makes me blush.

Edward's response to my painting has made me feel deceptive, even in my thoughts.

'I'm changing, that's all. Edward doesn't like it. It's confusing for both of us. He wants me to be the same Catherine forever. Basically he doesn't want me to paint.'

Cicely is quiet for a moment. 'I suppose you wanting to become an artist at your age is a bit overwhelming for him. Dear Catherine, you always were a bit of a dreamer. You don't want to jeopardise your marriage for a fad.'

'No,' I say.

My fifth morning in Paris. We are going to the Louvre. Geoffrey says I have to see the smiling lady. I am thrilled. For two days we have trudged around shops and I hated it. Cicely is in her element in shops and she chooses presents for everyone.

Now I stand in front of da Vinci's painting with fifty other jostling people. It's like being in yesterday's department store. Geoffrey and Cicely are deeply absorbed with each other and the smiling woman. I turn and hurry past the Old Masters, through a sculpture gallery, and then, oh joy, there they are. A room full of Renoir and Monet and Bonnard. Bonnard has broken all the rules. The edges of his pictures are bravely vivid and, in this one, the attention is drawn away from the woman in the centre. My body is alight and infuses with the colour. I am the gorgeous reds and oranges. I am paint. I am life. I am the dance that came before the first stroke of the paintbrush. I am in love with these paintings.

I know immediately it is him standing beside me.

'If I could paint, I would try to put your excitement in my picture. You are like a starved child who is given food. You are beautiful in front of this lovely Bonnard.'

'I am starved,' I say. 'I haven't been to a gallery for years and now that I am painting, I can't see enough. Learning about painting on your own is a lonely road, but thrilling too.'

'I would like to see your work. If it is as exciting as the way you look at Bonnard, then it will be good.'

I laugh. The light in the painting seems to be scattered in a strange enchanting way. It has a dream-like quality.

'Bonnard's use of light invites you into the picture. If this naked woman held out her hand to you, would you take it and allow her to draw you into her life?'

I think of my dream. Mr Renoir is in my head. He smiles.

I look into his eyes. 'Yes,' and I laugh again.

'Good day, Madame Bonnard.'

'Good bye, Mr Renoir.'

'Catherine!'

I turn to see Cicely watching us. She grabs hold of me as if I were a child and drags me away. 'Poor Edward! I just can't bear to think of poor Edward.'

Edward arrives and we spend a week enjoying French food and wine. We walk down narrow streets to discover little restaurants with daily menu changes that delight us. We do not mention Renoir, and Cicely is cool towards me.

Back in England, I dream again. I am modelling for an artist. His back is to me. I think it may be Bonnard, because I am surrounded by colour. I watch myself brushing my hair and see the reds and purples behind me. Then he turns and paints me and the light is bewitching. I am holding a muslin garment. The wind blows it and it moves gently. He paints my breasts and I feel my nipples tingling with the light. He touches my cheek softly. It is Mr Renoir.

Edward is shaking me. He wants to make love and is dragging me out of my dream. I hold onto wisps of it as we quietly have sex.

'It's so good to be home with my Catherine,' he says after he has come and lain back on his pillow. 'I miss you, darling, when you are away.'

Life continues as Edward likes it. Dinner parties, new recipes and the dining room redecorated. We go to London for the day and choose wallpaper. Monica comes to help me put it up. She asks about Paris. I describe the pleasure at seeing all those Renoir paintings and that exquisite Bonnard. My face is on fire I can feel it burning like a teenage blush.

'Is that all?' she asks. She tells me that Edward thinks I am involved with Rodney and has been asking her if it's true.

I laugh. Inside, I am furious. 'Why does everyone think I'm having an affair?' I ask.

She says it is because they see I have changed. 'You're not the same woman they all love. They think you're edgy and secretive.'

'Why must I always be what others want me to be? Why can I not be me?'

I feel like me when I paint. I feel strong and creative, even if the painting is not good. Life courses through my body. I fly with ideas through palettes of colour and imagination.

'Monica. What do you think?' I ask.

'You're ripe for a Mr Renoir,' she says.

I am working on many paintings. I am developing what Rodney calls a portfolio. I dream paint and images. I keep a diary of the process of my work and the dreams that I think I can use. In one entry, I write that I would like to dedicate the work to Mr R who inspired me. I sketch Mr Renoir on the steps holding his hand out to me. The picture unfolds. It is a fanciful piece, with vivid brushstrokes, rich in lust and hare-brained imagination. I show it to Rodney.

'It's time for you to go to London and show your work,' he says.

Monica and I go to the cinema one evening. Our friendship has grown with my need for dialogue about my work. We see a comedy and laugh and are feeling cheerful as we approach my house. I suggest she come in for a coffee.

The lights are out, which I find strange. I turn the key in the lock. Edward is standing just inside. He says goodnight to Monica in a commanding knife-slicing voice. Monica looks at me in alarm and leaves. I shut the door and Edward starts to cry.

'I can't believe what you are doing. How can you do this to me?'

I look around when he turns on the light. My paintings are scattered on the floor and taped to the walls are parts of my diary. The sketch of Mr Renoir has been given a place of precedence.

'If you were any good, it wouldn't be so bad. But you are prepared to make a fool of me with this rubbish. I told you I wanted you to stop this insanity. I gave you a holiday in Paris, but you pay me back with this. This is the influence of that dreadful fool Rodney. Is that who you were seen with in Paris? Did I pay for you to spend time with that idiot, that talentless moron?'

I cannot speak. I stand among the fragments of dreams and reality.

My work looks forlorn and hopeless in this state. I tell Edward I will never paint again. My heart is not beating. I have just vowed to take away its life force.

We go to bed. Edward makes love to me. I lie in his arms like a battered doll. My nice Edward, for whom I have slaved uncom-plainingly for twenty-four years. Edward, whom I suddenly can no longer love. We have shared so much but, as I go through the motions, I realise we have only shared his dreams, not mine. We entertain his friends, go to his favourite places on holiday and listen to his kind of music. I thought I liked it as well. Edward is particularly demonstrative in his lovemaking tonight and holds me down to kiss me so that I feel I am drowning. He wants me to do things we have never done before and my body feels violated.

'I love you, Catherine. Don't do this to me again. I love you.'

I dream again. I am flying. I am a kite and behind me there is a string on which are tied all my paintings. Edward is holding the rope and jerking me around the sky. He is angry and crying. A large bird is following me as I make patterns through the air. It pecks at me. I look down and see Mr Renoir. He takes the rope from Edward. Gently he pulls me in. My paintings pile up and I land on top of them. He wraps me up in a huge transparent blanket. I am cocooned and safe. He carries me into the Louvre and hangs all my paintings and then he puts me in a frame and hangs me on the wall. Crowds gather and look at me. The brushstrokes on my body illumine their faces.

In the morning, I gather up the paintings and torn pages from my diary. Monica rings and asks if everything is all right. I laugh. If sound has colour, my laugh is beige with brown edges. I will never paint again, I tell her. I telephone Rodney to say that I am not coming back to art class. He is very disappointed. He says he has arranged for me to meet a very well known art gallery curator in London. I tell him I can't go. I am burning my paintings. Rodney comes to the house with Felicity Peters, the vicar's wife. I am sitting still holding my paintings in my arms. He takes them all and leaves. Felicity tries to talk to me, but I can't respond. She leaves.

Edward comes back in the evening. He says nothing about the night before. We seem the happy couple we have always been, but I still cannot speak. He, as usual, does the talking. He plans a weekend in Scotland, near Edinburgh. I hear it all through a mist. Everything is foggy. Just as the telephone call is a few weeks later. It is Rodney. He tells me he has sent all my work up to a gallery. An exhibition is being organised. All I have to do is be there at the opening.

Monica comes to the station with me. At Waterloo, I hurry along the platform, take the underground and find the gallery. A familiar figure is there. I think I must be walking into one of my dreams.

'Hello, Madame Bonnard,' he says.

'Mr Renoir,' I gasp.

'Your exhibition is excellent. Yes,' he says looking at me start, 'Rodney contacted me and told me about this very talented painter. He showed me photographs. When I saw the use of light and colour, the thought did cross my mind, that it might be the same Madame Bonnard.'

I am so grateful.

My exhibition is critically acclaimed. Every paper talks about the new talent that has broken into the art world.

Edward comes home one evening with a newspaper in his hand.

'Did you read it?' I ask.

He nods.

'I can't not paint,' I tell him. 'If you don't want me to paint, then I am going to leave you, Edward.'

He nods again. I feel sorry for him. He is overwhelmed by his fear of my talent. Tears drip down his face. I turn and I walk away. If we stay together, we have to start again in a new way.

I dream that I am painting. Mr Renoir takes the brush from me and puts me into the frame again. He drags Edward to the painting. The two men stand and look at me and I look at them. Edward, who nearly destroyed me, and Mr Renoir, who saved me. I turn to a door in the painting and open it. I look back. They are still standing there. I close the door and find myself in a studio. I pick up a brush and look at an empty canvas.

For Suzanna
Waltz in the Rain

Bridget Grayson saw him after the very first concert of the string quartet. He was standing apart from the well-wishers and musical friends who had poured backstage. He was looking at her intensely.

She didn't go to the party being thrown for the quartet. Instead, she went to a café with him. He told her that during the concert he hadn't been able to take his eyes off her. He didn't hear a note of the music. Bridget laughed. He was witty and funny and she liked him.

In time, he introduced her to a life outside of music. She was typical of many artists who live for their art, sometimes a bit blinkered to the rest of world.

Nigel Lindsay was a successful businessman who worked for a large firm, travelled a lot and spoke two or three languages. Concert-going was his relaxation. Bridget and he enjoyed listening to music together and talking about it. They had fun. Before she met him, she was never very social. Her violin had been her constant companion, keeping her company during long solitary periods of practice. Nigel and the Quartet came into her life together.

The quartet was only recently formed. Bridget was the last player in as second violin. Maya was the leader and the creator of the quartet. She and Bridget had been at music school together. Maya chose the name Bacewicz for the quartet, after the Polish composer, Grazina Bacewicz. She said it didn't matter that no one would pronounce it correctly at first. They would get used to it. Her grandparents were from Poland. They had escaped from Cracow, where they had both been professional musicians, but their spirit was broken by the war. They taught music and remembered events about which they never spoke.

The quartet's debut had stamped its identity. As well as Beethoven and Schubert, they played contemporary or little-known Polish music. There was a healthy interest in their repertoire and they were busy.

Nigel and Bridget were married the next year in spring. The Bacewicz played as a trio during the ceremony in the local church. Nigel's humour made the reception memorable. He announced, through the haze of celebratory alcohol and with accompanying laughter, that now he was married he could take a mistress. 'Like a nineteenth century Frenchman,' he said. They were being photographed. Through her smiling, clenched teeth, Bridget said that she would kill him if he did.

'How?' he asked.

'With a knife,' she replied, 'that I'll keep sharpened for the purpose.'

They both burst into a fit of giggles and that photograph was the one that was framed and hung on the wall. It radiated happiness. Bridget was happy. The Bacewicz was in demand, and Nigel and she enjoyed each other's company.

After a particularly strenuous tour, the quartet returned to a period of no engagements. Nigel was away on business and Bridget missed him.

Maya telephoned to say she was planning an all-Polish concert of music from the early 1940s. Her enthusiasm spilled down the telephone. 'Bridge, will you help me? Help me find some quartets to play, so we can honour the musicians who weren't so lucky.'

When Nigel returned, he found Bridget absorbed in research. He helped her rummage through files in the library, where they unearthed a wealth of music that had been composed in Cracow during the war. They found writings and photographs. The images disturbed her. Dreams of war and music wove into a tapestry of expressive sound and fear.

Maya said they had enough material for a concert. Three quite different quartets. Of these, Bridget particularly liked the one called The Cracow. The composer had played the second violin part at the Cracow premiere, just before he was killed. She felt his fear and his love of life and marvelled at his courage as her bow hit the strings.

The concert went well. The audience was moved and the critics appreciative.

On the way home, Nigel said that a Polish friend had contacted him and wanted to visit them for a few days. 'If you have time, Bridge, get the place looking nice,' he said.

Bridget played her violin all morning then went to make the bed for Nigel's friend. It was then that she saw the book. A book of poetry inscribed with the words, 'Always yours, Nigel. We belong together. Come back to me soon. Macenka.' A photograph fluttered to the ground. It was a beautiful woman, voluptuous with high round breasts and a mouth that said, 'Come to bed with me.' Her large brown eyes smiled out at the camera. Behind her, Bridget recognised the statue of Adam Mickiewicz in the main market square of Cracow that she had seen in photographs. It was signed 'Macenka'.

Bridget took up her violin and played the beginning of a Beethoven sonata. The notes slipped and slithered into part of the lamenting slow movement of the Cracow Quartet and then to a discordant howl on the strings. She put the violin away and went to bed. Nigel crept in beside her when he returned from work. She turned her back to him.

Happiness, when it is shattered, is like a porcelain vase that falls from the table. The reason it falls is incidental, but the crash and ensuing sorrow is extensive. Bridget's happiness smashed like that. It happened first with the photograph and then with the arrival of Macenka.

Macenka burst into their lives, beautiful, as in the photograph. On the first evening, she asked for music and dragged Nigel to his feet. In front of Bridget, she took him in her arms and danced with him. He dissolved into a space in which only they existed. She watched like a voyeur as the dance transformed into warm sheets and open embraces. Nigel and Macenka danced with their hips stirring the embers that had held them close.

She felt the joy slide away from her like slippery skins.

At night, Nigel ceased to make love and called out in his dreams, 'Macenka.'

It was during one sleepless night that the man first appeared. He was standing at the window dressed in a tight suit and holding a violin case. He peered through the glass and smiled. She saw him again at the front door. He raised his hand in greeting. Then he entered the house, and sat in the corner of the kitchen from where he watched Bridget intently, whistling low when she looked at him. He took out his violin and played a melancholy tune.

Bridget lay in bed alone. Her body ached with bitter love. The violinist played a waltz and she imagined Macenka dancing, slowly turning-turning, her clothes falling to the ground. She ran her fingers over her own small breasts and pictured Nigel stroking Macenka. The violinist sat on the end of the bed. He struck the strings with his bow and she put her head under the sheets and held her ears. The agitated beat of the music vibrated in her body and she wanted to scream.

Bridget leapt from the bed when she heard Nigel laughing with Macenka. The strains from the violin became sultry and erotic. She danced towards them, spinning in jagged pirouettes, and struck Macenka hard in the face. Nigel looked at her, alarmed. His lips wet with kisses were not smiling. He grabbed Bridget and dragged her to the bedroom. He yelled. 'Macenka is our guest and you will apologise to her immediately.' She looked at the violinist, who shook his head.

Nigel had to go away on business. 'To Poland,' he said. 'Come with me Bridget, I'll show you Cracow.'

She didn't take her violin. She had stopped playing it when Macenka arrived.

Cracow was beautiful and stately. They walked across the main market square past the statue. Nigel put his arm around her shoulders and drew her towards him. He was holding her hand and laughing when she saw the violinist in a café and knew she was deceived. Macenka was not far away, but close on the heels of Nigel.

Later, she waited for Nigel in the hotel bedroom. Strains of a waltz in the street below caught her attention. She opened the window and saw Macenka and him together. Circling them was the violinist, hopping and prancing. He looked up and laughed and Bridget felt rage hit her with a punch in her belly. She ran down to the street. Macenka and Nigel looped arms and walked along the pavements oblivious of her.

For the succeeding days, Bridget trailed along from bar to restaurant watching them weave the strings of desire around each other. Sometimes the violinist walked beside her.

One evening, Macenka quarrelled with Nigel. Bridget and the violinist watched through the window as they leapt up from the restaurant table, plates of food tumbling to the ground. They ran out past them. Bewildered, Bridget followed, stumbling along rain-soaked pavements, where pools of light shone circles on her fear. At a bus stop, a crowd turned to look at her, voices whispering and curious. Some of them held violins in their hands, which they began to play. She screamed in terror and the beat of her own feet accompanied her tauntingly down a narrow alley. Behind her, the tap-tap of footsteps followed.

At the end of the alley lay an open space and an old building that might have been a church. Around it stood broken and leaning gravestones and in the light cast from a lamp she saw strange writing that she could not identify. Macenka and Nigel were kissing, held in a beam of light, absorbed in their passion. Bridget crouched behind a cracked stone and watched Macenka lift her skirt for him.

It was then that she felt unspeakable fury. She lunged towards them, but the violinist struck the strings of his instrument and a frenzy of notes sent her hurtling into a dance away from the feverish couple. The violinist took her in his arms. Bridget hummed the lamenting strains of the Cracow Quartet and he laughed. His thighs were against hers as he pushed her into the steps of a waltz. Her lips tasted of music and revenge and she sighed with desire for both. He took up his violin again. His fingers ran up and down the instrument. She stamped her feet and danced in agony and rage.

Madness comes in many forms. Sometimes the human heart cannot bear the hurt that another inflicts on it. Madness came to Bridget then. Maybe it had been there from the moment Macenka arrived. When she saw the violinist take a knife from his violin case, she knew it was a sign. He placed it ceremoniously into her hands and accompanied her steps with solemn chords that resonated in the dark cemetery.

Nigel turned and looked at Bridget as she approached. He reached out a hand as she raised the knife to plunge it into Macenka. In horror, he watched the blood spurt out. Macenka shook and trembled. Her sensuous face splintered in two. She crumbled into the rubble. The violinist took Bridget's hand and led her away from the cemetery. Behind her, she heard Nigel call her name. 'Bridget,' he called.

Bridget woke slowly. Dawn had crept through the curtains sending shafts of gold light across the bed. She shook off the cobwebs of her dream. Beside her Nigel slept, handsome and relaxed. A sense of fear gripped her.

She climbed out of bed and went to the kitchen and took a knife. Humming softly to herself she danced, weaving the knife in and out, partnering it in graceful turns. She spun widely arcing the knife. It sliced through the air and caught Nigel's cheek as he came through the doorway.

'My God, Bridget!' Nigel shouted. 'What the hell do you think you're doing?'

Bridget stood back. Blood dripped to the floor. 'I told you I'd keep the knife sharpened,' she said.

'Put it down, Bridge.'

She was trembling. 'Who's Macenka?' she asked.

'Macenka,' he echoed. 'Where did you get that name from?'

'The photo and the book. "We belong together."'

Nigel laughed nervously. 'Have you been going through my things?'

'Who is she?'

'She was,' he replied. 'You are. She is in the past.'

'Why didn't you mention her?'

'Why should I? As I said, she was and you are.'

Bridget pushed past Nigel and picked up her violin. She played the theme of the waltz from her dream.

Nigel stared at her aghast. 'How did you know that tune?' he stuttered.

'So it is true. It's the music that played in the street in Cracow.'

'Bridget, that was a long time ago.'

'Was it? Why do I know the tune, then?'

'Please stop playing it, Bridget. I love you. You know that.'

'And what about Macenka? And are there others? Do you love them too?'

He stepped towards her but she continued to play, her bow striking the strings harshly.

Nigel covered his ears and shouted, 'Stop, Bridge, for God's sake!'

She plucked the strings and stamped her feet and Nigel rushed at her and snatched the violin.

In the silence, she walked slowly to where she had dropped the knife. As she bent down, she heard the strains of the waltz and looked towards the window. The violinist grimaced and nodded. Nigel lowered Bridge's violin but the music was more frenzied.

'It's true!' she hissed between her teeth and the violinist smiled. 'You bastard.'

Bridget's violin fell from Nigel's hand and he looked at her with surprise, then horror as the knife penetrated his flesh. Louder, louder the music played. He staggered towards her and thought he saw a shadow pass the window.

The violinist smiled at Bridget, raised his hand and was gone.

Letters

My mother was a great letter writer. She wrote letters every week. On Sunday after lunch, she would sit and write to whichever family member was away. At first it was all of us, because we were all at boarding school. The letters were short and spoke of the essential, but were laced with the love that she found so hard to express in person. Always at the bottom was a kiss and hug written as X and O. There were often witty illustrations. She drew well and showed us her comical attempts to mow the lawn or make cakes. Her personal life and feelings remained a secret, though. If she had a whirling social life while we were away at school, there was no mention of it in her letters. It was as if her whole life was lived through her letters to us. In fact, she was better able to express her self in ink than in the spoken word.

Letters were a kind of lifeline to the place where my brother and two sisters shared our life by the sea, finding shells that sang, enduring games of Monopoly when it rained and having passionate fights over who should decorate the Christmas tree or not shut in the chickens at night.

There was no father in our life. He had gone away to Africa. Our parents lived a social illusion. They lived separately, on opposite sides of the world, my father initially on some diplomatic mission and then in a civil service job.

My mother told the curious that she did not follow her husband to Africa 'for the sake of the children's education'. 'I miss him so much,' she confided, 'but the children's future is important.' She appeared noble in her seclusion from normal married life.

I never questioned his absence, but I longed to be like other girls who had fathers who laughed and teased them and called them 'my little special girl'.'

My father's infrequent visits home from Africa were accompanied by tension that struck us dumb with anxiety. The undercurrent threat of violence and his inability to treat us as loved and respected children led us to feel like the remnants of a failed British Raj army. We did our best to avoid him and any dialogue that might invoke a rage.

My brother received the result of our ineptitude. When we caused a tantrum by some childish action or remark, it was to my brother that he turned to vent his spleen. We waited in the shadows of the night, hardly daring to breathe, to listen to my brother's silence as he was thrashed with my father's belt.

When he left to go back to Africa, we never spoke of him or cried to see him go. After one visit, we bought a dog, and that was the best exchange for our father. We watched his aeroplane take off into the sky and rushed to the kennels to return home with a tail-wagging soul that loved us and held us together as a family. Even when he ate my mother's best hat, we still embraced him. The dog taught us to love and touch and for him we longed for home. In the letters from our mother, she drew pictures of him as he grew into a dog as large as his paws had promised.

My brother was restless with all the female company. It was decided, maybe a command from my father – to give his son some male influence – to put my brother on to a ship to Africa. At our separate boarding schools our closeness had ebbed, and so we let him go.

My mother began writing her letters to him. Every week she wrote, 'My dearest, my darling son, How I miss you.' She poured out the love she had always felt, but had never been able to show to him. Each week, accompanied by sketches and anecdotes, the letters winged their way to Africa. My mother waited for a letter from him.

Months and months of lovingly worded letters remained unanswered. She continued to write but now with anxious pleas for a word. She looked at my brother's photograph. He gazed at her with hope and the hint of a smile. 'Why don't you write?' she whispered, and the silence resounded thunderously in empty response. The next Sunday she wrote a long, bitter letter.

Two weeks later, an aerogram arrived. Excitedly she opened the flimsy paper. A letter of blame and hurt. My brother accused her of never having cared. She only wrote to complain. Her bitterness offended him and he wanted nothing to do with her. He said, 'If you can't write anything kind to me, then don't bother at all. I've been away all this time and you can't think of a decent word to say to me. Please don't write again.'

She read the words with confusion and hurt.

My brother returned home after three years in Africa. He arrived, barely speaking. They looked at each other like enemies. Her resentment at receiving only coldness for her loving letters was an unspoken barrier between them. If she tried to tell him of her love, he ignored her. He believed she had sent him away more to be able to lavish love on his three sisters than for his good. It was proved by her acrimonious letters of criticism.

My father retired and returned a few years later as suddenly as he had left. Never very gracious in the art of relationship, he swept into the house and brought discontent and uncertainty with him. Once again, we children became members of his failed Raj army. Orders had to be obeyed and, if not carried out to his satisfaction, could cause a verbal temper or physical contact of fist and face. My brother was old enough to stay away; I don't remember him ever coming home at this time, nor did my mother write to him, except at birthday and Christmas.

My father died quite suddenly. He was angry and, as he stomped away from an argument, he had a heart attack.

In going through his desk, my mother found a tied bundle of opened letters. They were her letters to my brother. She parcelled them and sent them to him with a note. 'Here are the letters you never bothered to answer. You might want them as a record of your selfishness.' Love, the essential ingredient of most of the letters, was parcelled up, but my brother on reading the note, threw the parcel into a cupboard and forgot about it.

It was only when he moved house many years later that he came across the letters. My father had neatly and typically kept them in order of arrival. He opened the first letter and read, 'My dearest, my darling son, How I miss you. The place is so empty without you. I hate you being so far away.' The letters were full of love, sketches and amusing anecdotes at which he laughed, then cried. He read each letter several times. Tears poured down his face. How and why had he not received these letters in Africa? All the years had been wasted with resentment, jealousy and pain.

The truth was simple and unkind. My father had opened the letters. All those that expressed love and care he had withheld but for some perverse reason had kept neatly stored in his drawer. He allowed my brother to feel abandoned by his mother and his family. Whether his actions were against my mother, who loved her son as she did not love her husband, or against his son, who had not turned out to be the soldier man he wanted, will never be explained. That he did what he did was a terrible act, which destroyed the relationship between mother and son.

My brother wrote to my mother. He let his tears form the words of compassion, love and forgiveness. He talked of the sense of isolation he had experienced in Africa and the love he had always had for her. Eagerly he waited, but my mother never responded. Nor did she ever mention it. It was too late. The sorrow was too great and too ingrained.

My brother told the story to one of my sisters and it was she who later found his letter in my mother's desk after she had died.

She decided not to give it to him, but determined to burn it. 'It's all too late and too painful and it doesn't matter any more. But it's beyond me how anyone could do such a thing to their own blood,' she said to me.

This is the story of my brother's letters. Letters that were written with so much love but which produced only hurt and unhappiness.

Doorway

Rain. It's pouring. Got to stay in the doorway. Keep dry here. Invisible here. Dry and invisible. Need money. 'Excuse me, sir, got a dollar, have you?'

His look says it all.

You try being here. 'Not on drugs, sir. I'm trying to get my life back.'

Empty cigarette packet falls on the pavement near me.

He laughs.

Once, I laughed too. I had a home. A roof over my head. A sister who teased me. But then I heard these voices. They said odd things. I thought I was Jesus. My mum, single and hardworking, freaked. No one could stop the voices. On and on. I screamed, they screamed. They threw me out of school. I was disruptive, they said, and then Mum said she couldn't cope. She didn't want me to leave, but it was for the best. I wrote a few times, but not now. Look at me – grubby, homeless, sleeping in the park.

'Lady, you got a dollar, please, lady?'

She walks by. Looks familiar. Look down. Not good to look people in the eyes. Invites violence. Easy to be knocked about. Scared.

She stops. She's coming back. She kneels near me.

I smell bad, I'm sure.

'Don't I know you?' she asks.

'Don't think so,' I mumble. 'Just give us a dollar, lady.'

She takes ten dollars and puts it in my hand. The money connects us. She stays. I shut my eyes. She cries. I want to vomit, but I don't.

I open my mouth. One sound comes out. 'Mum.'

The Understudy

The hum of the audience stops. The musical director, 'the maestro', is making his way into the orchestra pit. I can imagine the spotlight catching him as he bows. The audience sits back in anticipation. My entrance is not for a long time yet, but on this night I want to be in the wings watching, getting the feel of it. I smell the scenery and make-up. The smell of theatre that I love.

The singer playing Angelotti is running across the stage gesturing wildly. Angelotti is an escaped political prisoner. He has come to the Church of Sant'Angelo for sanctuary. This Angelotti is Italian and known as Sisi. He speaks English, but never very much when it comes to acting techniques. To each direction he says, 'Si, si, I know. I do Angelotti many years.' His voice is strong and deep, but it's not enough in this modern world of opera only to have a good voice. Audiences expect reality of emotion and character. His saving grace is that he is kind, especially to young singers like me.

My throat is dry. I am waiting in the wings to sing my first Tosca, but I could be waiting to walk the high wire or jump off a cliff. Tonight, I, the understudy, am going on. Already the announcement has produced a gasp of disappointment from the audience. They are not on my side.

Yesterday I was told, not asked. 'Your big opportunity,' Cliff said when he rang me.

I was in the chorus until two years ago, and then moved up a rung to small parts and the occasional understudy of lead roles. Normally, though, they bring in another star to take over when a diva is ill. That way the audience is kept happy and the understudy is content to be in the shadow of a great singer.

***

A rehearsal was hurriedly organised. I know my music really well, as I'd been working on it every day. 'For the future,' I told my music coach. He arrived at the rehearsal beaming.

'You will be a beautiful and strong Tosca,' he said, embracing me.

I had been to most rehearsals and watched and listened, but it's quite different when you actually get up and do it. Stephen Tollander was helpful and generous. He's singing Mario Cavaradossi with a voice that is pure and expressive. It has a depth that is almost baritonal, but the high notes flow out easily too. He's come direct from a Covent Garden success.

He guided me from one move to the next and took me in his arms for the passionate moments in act one as if it were perfectly natural and I had always played the role. 'You'll be a great success,' he said kindly as he leant in to kiss me. 'Relax a little. You're a natural Tosca.'

'Thanks,' I stuttered.

***

The singer playing the sacristan is standing near me blowing his nose into his fingers and humming. Offstage he is a blustering man, wide-faced, unmusical, but with a character voice. He will continue to sing small roles until he dies. 'Break a leg!' he says as he stumbles on stage.

The audience laughs when they see him. His role of the sacristan gives credence to the church as a place of worship and some comic relief to a story that is unrelentingly tragic.

'Needs a singing lesson, or two,' I hear one of the chorus mutter.

My throat is drier. I ask for water.

The sacristan is singing with Cavaradossi. Stephen's generosity of spirit shines out in his voice. He is the right person to play the part of Cavaradossi the artist, who forfeits his life to help Angelotti escape. I watch him and imagine Tosca's passion for him that I will soon feel.

***

My rehearsal went well until the entrance of Scarpia. I have never liked Neville Stowe. He might be famous and a great baritone, but he's a mean man; vindictive and a womaniser. When I first joined the chorus, he bailed me up in the corridor and tried to kiss me. I pushed him away and his eyes lit up like the devil himself. I knew he'd never forget my response.

'You'll pay for it somewhere along the line,' advised my friend Olga. 'Men like that bide their time for their revenge.'

He came up behind me and sang, 'Tosca divina, la mano mia la vostra aspetta.' He should have been beside me to kiss my hand. I tried to turn into my next move, but he held my shoulders so that I faced away from the audience. His grip was intense.

'Mr Stowe, please let me go. You are hurting me,' I said as calmly as I could, but he gripped me harder.

The assistant director stopped the rehearsal. 'Geraldine, you should be stage left by now. You move on Scarpia's line, Un nobile esempio è il vostro.'

I went to kneel and heard behind me 'Couldn't they find a real soprano?'

I turned to him. 'I might not be a star right now, Mr Stowe, but I'm on the way up, not down.'

I heard the stage manager inhale through his teeth and the assistant director rushed in to give me the next move. The rehearsal pianist was smirking.

From the corner, a laugh erupted. 'Bravissimo! Eh, Neville. She talka lika la Diva vera!' It was Sisi.

Over lunch, Olga advised me to ignore him. 'When you've proved yourself, it'll be different.'

'That's great,' I said, 'when I'm about to sing my first Tosca without a proper rehearsal and with a man who seems to dislike me intensely. But it's not just that, Olga. I turned him down once and he hasn't forgotten it.'

'Ignore him,' she repeated, and I went to face the afternoon rehearsal.

Afterwards, I went home, flopped on my bed and slept. No gym. No TV. Healing sleep for tomorrow's challenge. I dreamt I was on stage in my costume in Scarpia's room. He was enjoying the torture of Cavaradossi and was making me listen to my lover's screams of pain from the dungeon. On the wall behind him there were photographs of beautiful women each dressed in Tosca's costume, the same as I am wearing right now while waiting to go on stage. In the corner there was an empty picture frame. Beneath was inscribed my name. I noticed the glass was broken as if it had been struck.

'You think you can make a fool of me in front of the cast. Well, I'll show you what I do to women like you.' He approached and put his hand on the back of my neck, twisting me to face him. 'You think you know what Scarpia wants. I don't want your body, my dear. But you will grovel before Scarpia is belittled.'

I struggled myself free and ran for the door. It opened to reveal the jailer, who told Scarpia that Cavaradossi was dead.

'That's not the story,' I shouted at Scarpia. 'I have to kill you first and then he dies.'

He laughed. 'Tonight we have a different version for you. I live long enough to accuse you of treason and from this window I watch you hang. No act three and beautiful duets with your lover. No throwing yourself off the balustrades. Instead, an ignominious death on the end of a dancing rope. A death suitable for an understudy.'

I woke with a start. The telephone was ringing.

It was Neville.

***

'Stand by, Miss Foord. This is your onstage call.'

The assistant stage manager, Tony, guides me to the church door.

I hear my music. 'Mario!' I sing, and think how Maria Callas moved the whole audience with this first word sung from offstage.

There is tension around me. Olga crosses her fingers in the air. Some of the chorus are standing in the shadows. Tony puts a thumb up and wishes me luck. I go through the door to face the audience. Stephen greets me as Cavaradossi. I am Tosca now and I am singing well.

Before I decided to become an opera singer, I had trained as an actor. That is one of my strengths and as I, Tosca, look around the church, I portray the jealous woman with a passion that I know is compelling. Stephen and I are singing as one. Our embraces are emotionally charged as if we were truly in love. Then I see the portrait he is painting. A beautiful blue-eyed blonde. My jealousy rises. The maestro is watching and supporting me. His eyes are alight with pleasure. The scene is over so quickly and it is time to exit.

'But paint those blue eyes brown,' I sing at the door and hear 'Bravo!' shouted from the audience.

Olga is waiting for me. I am shaking with excitement. 'You're doing brilliantly,' she says, giving me a squeeze.

Olga leads me to my dressing room, a small, soloist room. A large bunch of flowers from the management sits in a vase making it appear even smaller. My dresser hands me a glass of water and the make-up artist, Derek, rushes in to check my face. 'Sounds great, darling,' he says and flies out leaving a whiff of scent behind him.

I look at my score and go through my next music. I am trying not to think that it's Neville with whom I will share the scene.

***

'Can I come round?' he asked.

'I'm sleeping, Neville. I need rest.'

'I don't think you can do tomorrow without some help from me.'

'You're right there,' I said. 'But it would have been good to have had some help in rehearsals today. Isn't now a little late?'

'It's not yet seven o'clock.'

'I have a big day tomorrow, Neville.'

'You know, my dear, Scarpia has the power to make or break a Tosca.'

'I don't know how to take that, Neville.'

'Let me come round and explain.'

He must have been in the street, for he arrived within minutes. He brought a bottle of wine, a Merlot. I poured him some, and nursed a cup of chamomile tea myself.

He raised his glass. 'To Tosca.'

I sipped my tea and longed for sleep.

Neville rose and paced about the room, then came and stood behind me. He put his hands on the back of my neck. 'Scarpia holds Tosca, and pulls her gently to him. Of course, at first she struggles. But she realises how much depends on this moment. Scarpia says, Quest'ora io l'attendeva! Già mi struggea l'amor della diva!' and kisses her neck. Scarpia has waited a long time for this kiss. He has never been refused before.'

'Neville, you are not Scarpia now.'

'Does Scarpia frighten you, my dear?'

'No. Because he's not real, Neville. He is a character in a Puccini opera.'

He laughed. 'What would frighten you right now?' he asked.

I remained silent.

'Most divas dread the loss of voice. Tell me, little understudy, are you afraid of that? Or of a kiss from the lips of Scarpia?' His hands tightened on the back of my neck then moved slowly to grip my shoulders. 'Do you think Floria Tosca does not want Scarpia? Would it not empower her? Won't he be able to help her get what she wants in life?'

'I am Geraldine Foord, Neville. Tomorrow I am singing my first Tosca and I need rest.'

He continued as if I had not spoken. 'How do people get opportunities in life? How did you get this one, little understudy?'

I realised what he was accusing me of. It's true that I have played the game to the best of my ability. Tried to be seen and heard by directors and musical directors whenever I could. Sung in competitions and attended workshops. Been to see as many opera performances as possible. Read biographies and sung with small opera companies to gain experience. But I have never compromised myself in the way he was suggesting.

'This is your onstage call, Miss Foord.' The intercom sounds overly loud.

I rub the back of my neck.

In the church, I cannot find Mario Cavaradossi. Instead, Scarpia appears from the shadows. I am acting well and by the look on the maestro's face I know that musically I am pleasing him. Tosca is jealous when Scarpia shows her the fan belonging to the beautiful woman in the portrait, painted by her lover, Cavaradossi. I control Tosca's feelings and find a depth of despair that even surprises me. Neville is so slimy in the role, so evil, and if I didn't know better I would think he was acting, not just portraying himself.

'O che v'offende, dolce signora?' His eyes look sardonically into mine as he sings the line and strokes my cheek. That is not in the production. I see the assistant director in the wings signalling for me to move away, but Neville is holding my arm. Suddenly, he pushes me and I lurch across the stage to my knees. I fall awkwardly and feel pain shoot through my body. I can see he is quite out of control. The most important thing is to avoid physical contact. I dodge him dramatically and make it look like Tosca's insecurity. A butterfly caught in a cobweb. No one is smiling in the wings now. Olga looks really agitated.

At last I walk offstage. I want to burst into tears, but I must not let any one see how upset I am. If I cry, my singing will be affected. The voice is such a fragile instrument and stress does not benefit it. Olga takes me to my dressing room. She says nothing and I am relieved I don't want questions. Not till the evening is over. I still have two more acts to get through.

'Did you hear the audience?' my dresser says as she helps me out of my costume. 'They like you, love.'

I sip cold tea and breathe slowly.

The wig mistress tidies my hair. 'I hear it's going well, Geraldine. Well done.' She rests her hands gently on my shoulders and looks at the result of her work in the mirror. 'You'll do!'

***

'Take your hands off me, Neville,' I said.

'Violenza non ti faro. Sei libera.' Neville sang Scarpia's words softly.

The strength of anger rose in me and I leapt to my feet. 'I don't know what you want or what you're doing. You're totally out of order and I want you to leave. Now.'

'You have a debt to pay, my dear, and I thought you could pay this evening. I see I was wrong. A pity. It will have to wait for a less private time. I'm a patient man and an experienced Scarpia. I know every note, every bar, every word. I shall find the appropriate moment. And there's no point telling anyone about our little meeting. I shall say that you summoned me here to apologise for the comment you made this morning and you got worked up under the strain. They wouldn't want to lose a Scarpia, not for the sake of an unproven understudy.'

***

'Geraldine!' my dresser is holding out my costume. I stare at my face in the mirror. 'You look lovely, dear.'

My eyes look back at me with apprehension. Lovely is not what I need, but strength and cunning and vocal ability.

Derek dashes in and powders my face with a flourish. 'Darling, I hear you are sensational. Never doubted it myself.'

My eyes give me away.

'Are you all right, darl?'

'She's fine,' says Olga before I have time to reply.

I look at her and I see her worried face transform to a supportive smile. I step into my costume. Derek flicks some powder off my shoulder and skips out of the room.

'He pushed me, Olga,' I say as we walk down the corridor.

'Yes. I saw.'

'He's mad. I'm scared.'

'You can't afford to be, Geraldine. You are Tosca now and she is brave and strong. And you're singing brilliantly tonight. Go be Tosca.' She squeezes my hand.

Olga and I joined the chorus at the same time and she, like me, has become a minor soloist. She is a good friend and, right now, I need her.

I walk to the side of the stage. Neville has just finished Scarpia's big aria. He turns away from the audience and pours himself some wine, then glances towards me in the wings. I feel a chill go through my body. He is ignoring Cavaradossi, who has been brought in for questioning, and, although he sings Scarpia's music, he keeps his eyes on me. I take a breath, mutter a quick prayer and walk into the scene.

Stephen looks handsome and heroic. He bravely denies knowledge of the escaped prisoner and laughs at Scarpia. The guards drag him to the dungeons to be tortured. Neville still watches me like a cobra.

The production demands that Tosca keep her distance at first. I stay further away than I should, but just within my light. I remove my gloves and elegant boa. Scarpia sits at his desk, sipping his wine. He asks me where Angelotti is hidden. I refuse to tell him. Cavaradossi howls in pain from below. In the wings I see the Assistant Director signalling me to move nearer to Neville. I ignore him. If I stay where I am standing, I will get through the scene. This moment between Scarpia and Tosca is so powerful. He wants to have sex with Tosca, but he also wants to destroy her. He knows how to pull her into his net. He says that he will stop the torture if Tosca will tell him where Angelotti is hidden. Finally, and desperately, after a long agonised howl from the dungeon, 'In the well, in the garden,' I tell him.

Mario Cavaradossi is released. Stephen staggers onto the stage, his face bloodied from the torture. I feel so much love and passion for him, but he pushes me away when he discovers that I have revealed Angelotti's hiding place. He is taken offstage by the guards leaving Neville and me alone.

I wish at this moment that Puccini's opera had a different storyline and I could be singing with Cavaradossi right now, not Scarpia. I see

Stephen stop in the wings. Sisi is saying something to him. He looks over his shoulder at me. There is nothing he can do.

Scarpia offers me a seat and I lower myself gracefully. I beg and implore him to save Cavaradossi. Neville watches me, his eyes hard.

My famous aria approaches. The maestro is looking at me. I stand and he raises his baton.

'Visi d'arte, visi d'amore.' I love this aria so passionately. I know that I can sing it beautifully.

Out of the corner of my eye, I see Neville get to his feet. He is walking slowly towards me. The high B flat is coming up and I need all my strength. I know what he's going to do, and he does. He puts his hand on the back of my neck. His fingers dig into my skin. For a moment, I feel the same terror of last night, then I remember that I am Tosca. I pull myself away from his grip and sing as I never did before and the note comes out clear as a bell.

The audience cheers and the maestro beams. We continue the scene.

I kneel at Scarpia's feet. Tosca is almost ready to give up her fight. It is a touching moment. Suddenly, Neville lunges towards me and I throw myself sideways. I know if I keep my diaphragm under control I shall still be able to sing. He grabs my arm and raises me to my feet into an embrace. Usually, operatic embraces allow an openness to let the voice out to the audience, but he is holding me so tight that I can't turn to them. I push my hands into his chest to avoid being crushed. The audience must think this is very real, and it is, except I'm not acting. I am fighting for my right to sing.

I wonder, if I had allowed Neville to kiss me all those years ago in the corridor, whether this would be happening.

Neville will have to let go soon. He has to write the letter for Tosca, giving safe passage of escape for her and Cavaradossi. He releases me roughly and I stumble backwards, but I am still on my feet.

Neville sits at Scarpia's desk to write the official letter. I look around and see the knife on the table behind him. I pick it up. Tosca has to stab Scarpia. 'Tosca, finalamente mia!' he sings. But I am already afraid. The knife is not the prop it should be, but a real knife, sharp and pointed.

I raise my hand, but Neville turns and grabs my wrist.

I am singing, 'This is how Tosca kisses!', which is when I should kill him. Instead, he takes the knife and is wielding it at me, slashing at my cheek. Blood runs down my costume.

'Ti soffoca il sangue,' I sing, trying to push him away and to wipe the blood off my face. He holds my wrist. With all my strength, I swing in and kick him as my brother once taught me 'if you're being bothered by a man.' Neville falls to the floor groaning and I push him over.

I take the two candelabra and place them on either side of him. The letter should be in his hand, but his change of production has hidden it. I search desperately for it and find it by his head.

As I bend to pick it up, Neville mutters, 'I haven't finished with you yet.' Just the crucifix needs to be laid across his chest. I kneel. 'Listen to the audience, Scarpia. Let them be the judge.'

As I make my exit, the first Bravo! rings out and is followed by a chorus that fills the house.

In my dressing room, I am almost hysterical with relief that I do not have to sing with him again. My shoulders are bruised, my lower back hurts from the fall and I have a thin cut on my face. There is a knock on the door.

Stephen strides in and hugs me. 'You were spectacular! Even the bits you made up were a real plus. Geraldine, you won't do anything so dramatic in the next scene with me, though, will you?' He is trying to smile and make light of it.

'No, Stephen. I don't volunteer for these sort of bruises every day.' My tone makes it clear that I resent his flippancy.

He looks at me with concern.

'Don't say anything.' I try to sound calm. 'Just go and sing your aria divinely.'

He stops at the door. 'Sorry, Geraldine,' Then, 'He's a bastard!' he exclaims softly with his back to me and leaves.

Derek rushes in. 'Everybody is raving. Geraldine, you were sensational with Scarpia. Tony said it looked like a real fight. Oh theatre, how I love you!' He gives a little jump and flutters out of the dressing room.

I can hear the third act beginning. The strains of 'E lucevan le stelle' are pouring into the room. I feel Stephen is singing for me. That Puccini wrote the aria for me.

Tony knocks on the door and suggests I look at the mattresses where I have to jump at the end of the scene.

'Olga, come with me.' I am still shaking a little and she takes my hand.

We walk together to the pile of mattresses that has been placed below the balustrades. I've only had one opportunity to practise, so I look and imagine myself jumping safely.

The third act is wonderful to sing. As soon as I am on stage, I forget the last dreadful scene with Neville. The music holds me, embraces me. Puccini excelled in it. It is dramatic, hopeful, desperate and full of love. I feel I can really let go with Stephen. There is nothing to fear. He is singing to me with so much emotion. It is electric. Tosca is in love with him and my heart is brimming with intense feeling.

Earlier, in front of Tosca, Scarpia had instructed his henchman, Spoletta, to arrange a pretend execution. Tosca is unaware she is being betrayed. She is so sure she has a future with her beloved Mario. The guard says it is time and right to the end I show Mario how to play-act and feign death. The soldiers raise their rifles. They aim and fire. When they have gone, I run to him and tell him it is time to escape, but he is dead. Scarpia has won.

His murdered body is discovered and the soldiers rush in to arrest me. I have only one place to go. I have to jump off the balustrade to the ground below. I run to the edge and look for the pile of mattresses. It has been moved away from the set. I will really have to leap if I am to reach it. Standing in the middle of the top mattress is Neville. He is holding the knife. Lying on the floor beneath him is the stagehand who is supposed to help me down. I can't believe that nobody has seen Neville. And where is Tony?

'O Scarpia,' I sing. 'Avanti a Dio!'

The assistant director is windmilling me to jump. He might burst. Olga rushes towards the mattresses. I wonder if they will bring the curtain down and the critics will write derisively about the Tosca who would not jump.

I hear someone shout, 'No! No!' It is Sisi. He is climbing up the mattresses and has taken hold of Neville. 'You jump, Signora!' he cries. And I do.

The curtain comes down and I lie on the mattresses and cry. Olga helps me down.

Derek powders my tear-streaked face as I am propelled to the wings to wait for my curtain call. 'Sensational! Darling!' he calls after me as I walk into the light and stand centre stage.

Aunt Phoebe

A knock on the door coincided with the first dawn light squeezing through the curtains. Footsteps, a cup of tea. If my eyes were shut, I could smell her scent, an aroma redolent with love and safety. I opened my eyes. Aunt Phoebe was already dressed and looking beautiful. She never wore conservative clothes, but they were expensively cut and designed and very colourful. She opened the curtains to reveal a grey sky and asked me my plans for the day.

'Mmmm.'

She kissed me on the forehead. 'Do you want me to run a bath?'

I nodded, but cuddled down into the warmth of dreams and sleep. From the bathroom, I heard the water running. Aunt Phoebe lived in a small house in which the bathroom was one of the larger rooms. Beside the bath there was a small table on which stood a pile of books and a telephone. My aunt liked to soak in the evenings with a good book and have the telephone handy for long conversations about recent publications or ideas she was incubating. There were always flowers there too.

She wasn't married and some people might have pitied her, imagining her to be lonely, but she lived a social life that was both fun and interesting. She certainly wasn't short of gentlemen who took her to concerts and exotic restaurants, nor of women friends, most of whom were 'brainy', as my mother described them with a curl of her lip. She was always doing something interesting and found time to write highly successful books and volumes of poetry.

My mother was born seven years before my aunt. It seemed that the disparity of years had given my aunt a propensity for love of life but had blessed my mother with neither benevolence nor a sense of fun.

In a marriage, clamorous with unspoken resentment, my mother performed charitable works that gave her standing in the community and pushed my doctor father towards ambitions that were not of his dreams. He was a small-town GP, popular with his patients for his kindness and care, happy with country life and with little appetite for my mother's vision of him as an important medical expert.

It was a relief to leave home for university. My mother's face had squeezed tight as if she were sucking a lemon when I had told her that Aunt Phoebe had invited me to stay until I found suitable accommodation.

'If she lives with Phoebe, she'll turn out like her. No good for any man. Too much brain and too little sense.'

'Phyllis,' for once my father spoke, 'she's grown-up now. She can decide what she wants for herself.'

Aunt Phoebe had said it was important to do what you really want, otherwise life is a waste. 'Have a passion for whatever you do,' she always advised me. 'Come and stay with me for a few months until you've made friends.'

The thought of having friends without them being judged by my mother was overwhelmingly tempting. I thought of the day I'd been given a lift home by a boy I knew from school; not a boy friend. My mother grilled him; school, parents, job aspirations. She decided he was not 'our sort' and wanted to frighten him away. I had sat in a corner humiliated. He saw the funny side, though, and burst out laughing and made up a story fit for any snob. I met my friends elsewhere after that and warned those who were intrepid enough to venture over our threshold to have a sense of humour.

'You'll meet all the wrong sort of people with Phoebe,' my mother warned, 'not the sort who will do your father's work any good nor your career, my girl.'

'Oh, Phyllis, do leave her alone.'

'Well, I can warn her, can't I? Remember, I know what Phoebe is really like.'

'It's only for a few months,' I said lamely to my mother's back as she went into the kitchen where an orchestra of utensils expressed her prejudice with percussive sounds that echoed on the walls. They filled every corner of the house, pushing me towards the door.

I joined my father in being the recipient of unspoken, angry words. He looked at me with kind eyes and shrugged. There was something he wanted to say, but instead of speaking he kissed me and went out into the garden. I watched him bending over a bed of sweet williams. He was always content amongst flowers and they grew for him in colourful abundance.

A few days later, I left for Aunt Phoebe's. We were both comfortable in each other's company and the months stretched out until I didn't want to live anywhere else. The combination of university and the freedom of her way of life was liberating after the stifling atmosphere of home.

My aunt had not been to university, despite a penchant for literature and an ability to write. My grandparents thought she would be better off going to secretarial college. There she spent little time in the classroom, preferring to be out on the street protesting against the Vietnam War, which was raging at the time. She joined peace marches and experienced exhilaration from the melting pot of classes and cultures that joined her to sit silently outside embassies or march across the city in youthful rebellion. She began to write poetry, at first naïve love verse, but later well crafted political statements and poems of social conscience. As the war grew more intense, she kept a diary in which she wrote what she saw during the protest marches. Crowds gathering, police nervously pushing them, a policeman's helmet snatched and thrown into the air. Young people singing. A man tossed into a fountain. Children screaming. A woman falling underfoot. A group at prayer. A busker wildly strumming a guitar. Her poems were economical like Japanese writings and she accompanied each verse with a cartoon illustration.

Her book was published and sold out and reprinted. My favourite poem was called 'Cynical wit in rhythm with falling bombs', not because of its poetic value, but because I could imagine my aunt striding down the street shouting and singing and believing she was changing the world. I could see her face intense with emotion and everyone around her moved by her exuberance.

She had an infectious effect on most people whom she met. Smiles seemed to stretch wider and laughter be heard more. Only my mother threw herself into guerilla tactics whenever the two of them met. It was my aunt's encroachment into an intellectual world, in which she had no right, having not received a university education, that set off my mother's alarm bells. My aunt's literary works were on the academic syllabus of many leading tertiary institutions, and my mother said that, although it was obviously an achievement, it didn't say much for the standards at universities.

Visits to our family were a duty that Aunt Phoebe stoically performed. She entered our neat and dull household in which a dent in a cushion could cause concern. After twenty minutes, the tense atmosphere lightened. 'Duty done!' she whispered. My mother waited for an opportunity to criticise Aunt Phoebe, but her pointed remarks elicited laughter. If my aunt was upset, she never let any of us know.

The last visit was at Easter. Phoebe had driven me. On the way, she told me about her latest publication. She said it was, 'between the two of us', somewhat autobiographical. 'Oh dear,' I thought. 'Mum's not going to like it.'

We were sitting around the dinner table, full from a delicious meal that made up for the Lenten fast. We had guests and one of them mentioned the book and how much he had enjoyed it. I wished I'd read it so that I could appreciate the conversation.

'You made the love affair so real. Excellent reading! Couldn't put it down. I felt I was reading an account of something very personal. I suppose that's what makes you creative people tick. You use your imagination to great effect.'

Phoebe thanked him. He asked if anyone else had read it.

I was surprised to discover that my mother had. She started to pull the book to bits like a literary critic. Phoebe sat quietly as the conversation became lively. My mother's voice had a metallic sound to it. Usually I switched off when my mother was holding court, but her tone alerted me. I tried to interrupt and change the subject. Something warned me that she was leading us to an ugly scene.

It was my father who saved the moment. 'Phyllis, this is Phoebe's work. She should be allowed to leave it behind and rest from it occasionally. Now, what about a spot more wine.' And my father led the conversation away from Phoebe.

When the guests had left, I heard my mother in the kitchen. Whether she was directing her gunfire at the saucepans or my father was not clear. Her voice sliced through the air and my aunt and I sat in front of the television pretending not to hear.

'Personal experience, he says? Imagination! All she ever had was a string of sordid student affairs that shamed our family and led our mother to an early grave. How dare he imply that she might be an authority on love? Love is between decent people who hold certain moral codes sacred. Any other sort is just whoring. But it's not surprising that she should write a book like this.'

I heard my father's quiet voice trying to reason with her, then silence. The door opened and his footsteps dragged up the stairs. She followed him out and shouted up, 'And the man in her book is married. How can people think it's a good read? Married!'

The door flew open.

'How dare you write about this sort of thing when it's so immoral? Do you ever think of the impact your writing has on our lives?'

'Mum, it's only a story!' I said, but at the back of my mind I remembered Phoebe saying that it was 'somewhat autobiographical'. She wanted me to know. Why?

'And one that will make me and your father the laughing stock here. She's flaunting adultery at us.'

'Mum. Shakespeare wrote *Othello*. It didn't mean that he was either black or a murderer.'

Phoebe sat looking down at her hands. Her breathing was shallow. She was biting her lip.

'I wouldn't put it past you to have an affair with a married man. You always were a law unto yourself without any thought as to other people's feelings.'

'Phyllis,' Phoebe spoke at last, 'you're like a bothersome wasp that won't go out of the window but keeps buzzing.' She spoke without moving, her eyes still lowered. 'You must be hell to live with.'

I turned and looked at my mother. She was staring at Phoebe with hate in her eyes. I got up to go to her, but she quickly went through the door and shut it behind her. Phoebe still sat quite motionless.

The stairs creaked and the door slowly opened. My father stood in the doorway. He was ashen, his face twisted in grief. 'I'm sorry,' he said.

'Daddy, darling, you didn't do anything to apologise for,' and I went to him to put my arms around him.

He hugged me, but his attention was not on me. He held out a hand to Aunt Phoebe and she came towards us. We stood there, the three of us, silent for a long time.

'I have to go to bed,' he said and shut the door behind him.

I turned to Aunt Phoebe and saw she was crying.

'No words,' she said and sat down and continued to look at her hands.

The next day I felt compelled to buy a copy of the book and find out why it had caused so much strife. My mother's reaction was so emotionally charged. More than her usual upholding of dreary middle-class values.

I was enthralled by what I read. It was a tender, beautifully written story about an affair that had started when the couple was already middle-aged. They had bumped into each other on a train, had started talking and become so involved in words and ideas that they had stayed on beyond their individual destinations. Phoebe made the train journey a kind of allegory to the real-life event, which was the realisation that this was the love of their lives and his marriage, a banal tragedy. They travelled to Paris, not together, but separately, and met in a small hotel where they were anonymous. There they made love for the first and only time and he threw off the constraints of unhappiness and for a few days forgot about his wife and his dull marriage. They went to art galleries and a concert and kissed in a narrow street leading to the Louvre. A young man whistled at them and they laughed at the situation as only those can who have left youth behind.

The train journey was one of many that they took. They played a game pretending they were meeting for the first time. They knew that the other passengers would be listening, and it heightened the pleasure of desire and passion to weave intricate stories about themselves. He always took flowers from his garden with him and before they reached the station he would lean forward and hand them to her.

The train journeys were like sunsets that touched the soul and overcame the darkness and tedium of every day life. It was perfect. One day she failed to turn up and he sat in the train alone with his bunch of flowers. It signalled the end of the affair. The reader was left wishing them together, wanting the fairytale ending.

I thought of my mother and wondered if it was she who was the wife in the banal marriage. Surely, Phoebe wouldn't do that. I was overcome with compassion, but I knew that any feelings I might show to my mother would be received with her usual disdain.

I tried to speak to Phoebe about her book but she laughed and made light of it. 'If you want to know more, come and hear me speak about it tomorrow evening. There's a writers' forum. It'll be boring as can be, but you're welcome.'

The hall was full. It was obvious that the book was popular. I was proud to hear her speak, and the many questions from admiring readers.

'Miss Taverner, do you base your stories on personal experience?' A young woman was standing.

My aunt smiled. 'Everything we write has something to do with our own experiences, even if it is not directly about them. An historian will write history from his or her own bias, because it is understood from the platform of his upbringing and experiences. But we do, as creative writers, have the opportunity to use our imagination and put ourselves into certain situations as if we were living them first hand.'

'You talk a lot about flowers in your book. Is horticulture a hobby?'

'Some men find growing flowers the only method of escape from the tedium of life as it is. I used the garden as a metaphor.'

I thought of my father bending over the sweet williams in the garden. He certainly had been escaping. He loved flowers. I remembered him saying to me as a child that love was like a flower, brilliant and sweet at first.

Not long after, my aunt decided to go abroad and she left quite suddenly. I had a whole house to myself. I missed her, but university work and a waitressing job kept me occupied. Sundays were best. I'd curl up on the sofa and read books or listen to music. Every room had one or two floor to ceiling bookcases overflowing with months of reading. Authors of whom I'd never heard, and old and much loved ones. A bookcase of poetry lured me and I read ee cummings and Auden, Donne and Herrick. I love poetry and for days I read and recited out loud, enjoying the music of the words. An anthology caught my eye. I pulled it out to see if it had any of Aunt Phoebe's work in it. There was an inscription written in a familiar hand,

> Beloved, thou has brought me many flowers
> Plucked in the garden all the summer through
> And winter, and it seemed as if they grew
> In this close room, nor missed the sun and showers.
>   – Elizabeth Barrett Browning
>
> The flowers I bring you are as nothing to those you give me.
> My love always.

I skipped through the pages to see if there were any other clues, but I knew the answer.

I didn't know what to do. If there was anyone I could talk to. If it was indeed my business at all. I felt cold and confused. I went to bed and my sleep was sporadic and unsettled. But I did sleep because I dreamed. I was on a train and was surrounded with flowers. He was sitting opposite me. He saw my confusion and he cried. 'You don't understand.' We stopped at a station and my mother got into the carriage. I wanted to tell her what had been going on, but the flowers were wilting and that worried me. He leant forward and said, 'Love keeps the flowers beautiful.' I woke up.

The telephone was ringing. It was my mother. 'I need you to come home.' Her voice was shaking.

'Mum, what is it?'

'Just come home.'

I took the first train.

She opened the door to me looking her usual self, which was disturbing, considering only a few hours before she had sounded so agitated. I wondered what the crisis might be that had caused her to demand my immediate presence.

'Your father is in hospital,' she informed me dryly. 'He's had a stroke.' She went into the kitchen and I waited for the saucepans to crash, but there was nothing but a deafening silence.

I followed her, wanting to know more. She was sitting at the table, back erect, twisting a tea towel in her hands. I put my arm around her shoulders. I thought she was crying, but when she turned her face to me I saw it was twisted in crooked laughter.

'He thought I didn't know,' she spat the words out. 'He thought I didn't notice the flowers and the train journeys and the look on his face when he came back – from her. The moment she was born she brought nothing but trouble to us. And she got everything on a silver spoon. Then this, the book informing the entire world about him and her. So I told him, I told him to give her up or get out of this house. He couldn't make a decision, just like in the book. He tried to tell me that he had never had sex with the bitch, but I know her better. Women always know. He's a weak man. He took the coward's way out through the hospital door. Well, let him lie there in his self-pity. I'm clearing out his things and he can look to her for sympathy.'

Her anger and distress were dreadful. She could not see, nor make allowance for, all the years of bullying, putting my father down, shouting at him. She had made the house into a sterile showpiece in which love had been misplaced. She had driven him towards ambitions that were not his, always wanting more and more from him. Her relentless domineering pushed him through the door into the arms of another woman and now she wanted revenge.

My father lay in the white hospital sheets looking small and pathetic. His mouth was twisted and one eye was sagging, but he could speak slowly. I stroked his cheek. It was wet. He had been crying.

The words came with difficulty. He told me how he had hardly known Aunt Phoebe, she being so much younger than my mother. On her occasional visits, he was usually too busy seeing patients to spend much time socialising with her. Then they met on a train.

'I laughed with her. And I talked and she listened. She didn't speak about her aches and pains, which is what I hear all day, nor about what I don't achieve. We spoke of poetry and books and music and God and flowers, and flowers and flowers.' His voice tailed off. He took a breath. 'We made garlands of our words. We played games, just like in the book, so that we could weave new strings of language and love.'

'What about Paris, Dad?'

'She made that up. We never made love, only with words. That was the wonder of it. I wanted to, of course. But this love was soul food. It was my heaven.' He shut his eyes.

'And Mum is your hell,' I kissed him and went back to my mother.

She was fiendishly packing, throwing my father's life into boxes. China was shattered on the floor, shirts in with books. I took hold of her and shook her. She stared at me with dazed eyes.

'They didn't make love.'

'I don't care.'

'But it's important. It wasn't an affair. It was a friendship.'

'It was love.' She spat the words out as if they contained poison. 'He loved her.'

'This has nothing to do with Dad, does it? It's to do with Phoebe. You're jealous of her, so you're going to punish Dad for it. She managed to be successful, and to be free. You hate her for her free spirit and the way that everyone loves her so much.'

Now that I had started, I couldn't stop. 'You never listened to Dad. You just complained at him. You took no interest in his love of flowers, but she did. You wanted him to be everything and anything he wasn't. She accepted him as he was. You took him to the door. In fact, Mum, you took him to the station and put him on the train.'

I'd said enough, too much. She sat crumpled on the floor beside a packing box.

'Perhaps it's your life you should be tidying up, Mum, not his.'

I went upstairs and collected my bag. I was tired of being in the middle of an emotional roundabout. Three people pulling themselves into a vortex.

When I came down, Mum was at the front door. We looked at each other. I saw she had been crying, but she said nothing. I went to her and took her in my arms. For some time she remained there, but when the front door bell rang she wiped her face and opened the door to the taxi driver, composed and seemingly cold again.

I got into the taxi. As it sped away, I looked back. The front door was already closed.

www.ingramcontent.com/pod-product-compliance
Lightning Source LLC
Chambersburg PA
CBHW020348110726
47898CB00003B/1089